The Kepi

If I remember rightly, I have now and then mentioned Paul Masson, known as Lemice-Térieux on account of his delight – and his dangerous efficiency – in creating mysteries. As ex-president of the Law Courts of Pondichéry, he was attached to the cataloguing section of the Bibliothèque Nationale. It was through him and through the library that I came to know the woman, the story of whose one and only romantic adventure I am about to tell.

This middle-aged man, Paul Masson, and the very young woman I then was, established a fairly solid friendship that lasted some eight years. Without being cheerful himself, Paul Masson devoted himself to cheering me up. I think, seeing how very lonely and housebound I was, he was sorry for me, though he concealed the fact. I think, too, that he was proud of being so easily able to make me laugh. The two of us often dined together in the little third-floor flat in the rue Jacob, myself in a dressing gown hopefully intended to suggest Botticelli draperies, he invariably in dusty, correct black. His little pointed beard, slightly reddish, his faded skin and drooping eyelids, his absence of any special distinguishing marks attracted attention like a deliberate disguise. Familiar as he was with me, he avoided using the intimate '*tu*,' and every time he emerged from his guarded impersonality, he gave every sign of having been extremely well brought up. Never, when we were alone, did he sit down to write at the desk of the man whom I refer to as 'Monsieur Willy' and I cannot remember, over a period of several years, his ever asking me one indiscreet question.

Moreover, I was fascinated by his caustic wit. I admired the way he attacked people on the least provocation, but always in extremely restrained language and without a trace of heat. And he brought up to my third storey, not only all the latest Paris gossip, but a series of ingenious lies that I enjoyed as fantastic stories. If he ran into Marcel Schwob, my luck was really in! The two men pretended to hate each other and played a game of insulting each other politely under their breath. The *s*'s hissed between Schwob's clenched teeth; Masson gave little coughs and exuded venom like a malicious old lady. Then they would declare a truce and talk at immense length, and I was stimulated and excited by the battle of wits between those two subtle, insincere minds.

The time off that the Bibliothèque Nationale allowed Paul Masson assured me of an almost daily visit from him but the phosphorescent conversation of Marcel Schwob was a rarer treat. Alone with the cat and Masson, I did not have to talk and this prematurely aged man could relax in silence. He frequently made notes – heaven knows what about – on the pages of a notebook bound in black

The Kepi

Colette

A Phoenix Paperback

The Kepi first published in *Le Képi* by Fayard in 1943.
Taken from *The Collected Stories of Colette*
published by Secker and Warburg 1984.

This edition published in 1996 by Phoenix
a division of Orion Books Ltd
Orion House, 5 Upper St Martin's Lane, London WC2H 9EA

ISBN 1 85799 758 1

Typeset by Deltatype Ltd, Ellesmere Port, Cheshire
Printed in Great Britain by Clays Ltd, St Ives plc

imitation leather. The fumes from the slow-burning stove lulled us into a torpor; we listened drowsily to the reverberating bang of the street door. Then I would rouse myself to eat sweets or salted nuts and I would order my guest, who, though he would not admit it to himself, was probably the most devoted of all my friends, to make me laugh. I was twenty-two, with a face like an anemic cat's, and more than a yard and a half of hair that, when I was at home, I let down in a wavy mass that reached to my feet.

'Paul tell me some lies.'

'Which particular ones?'

'Oh, any old lies. How's your family?'

'Madame, you forget that I'm a bachelor.'

'But you told me . . .'

'Ah yes, I remember. My illegitimate daughter is well. I took her to lunch on Sunday. In a suburban garden. The rain had plastered big yellow lime leaves on the iron table. She enjoyed herself enormously pulling them off and we ate tepid fried potatoes, with our feet on the soaked gravel . . .'

'No, no, not that, it's too sad. I like the lady of the library better.'

'What lady? We don't employ any.'

'The one who's working on a novel about India, according to you.'

'She's still laboring over her novelette. Today I've been princely and generous. I've made her a present of baobabs and latonia palms painted from life and thrown in magical incantations, mahrattas, screaming monkeys, Sikhs, saris, and lakhs of rupees.'

Rubbing his dry hands against each other, he added: 'She gets a sou a line.'

'A sou!' I exclaimed. 'Why a sou?'

'Because she works for a chap who gets two sous a line who works for a chap who gets four sous a line, who works for a chap who gets ten sous a line.'

'But what you're telling me isn't a lie, then?'

'All my stories can't be lies,' sighed Masson.

'What's her name?'

'Her Christian name is Marco, as you might have guessed. Women of a certain age, when they belong to the artistic world, have only a few names to choose from, such as Marco, Léo, Ludo, Aldo. It's a legacy from the excellent Madame Sand.'

'Of a certain age? So she's old, then?'

Paul Masson glanced at my face with an indefinable expression. Lost in my long hair, that face became childish again.

'Yes,' he said.

Then he ceremoniously corrected himself. 'Forgive me, I made a mistake. No was what I meant to say. No, she's not old.'

I said triumphantly: 'There, you see! You see it *is* a lie, because you haven't even chosen an age for her!'

'If you insist,' said Masson.

'Or else you're using the name Marco to disguise a lady who's your mistress.'

'I don't need Madame Marco. I have a mistress who is also, thank heaven, my housekeeper.'

He consulted his watch and stood up.

'Do make my excuses to your husband. I must get back or I shall miss the last bus. Concerning the extremely real Madame Marco, I'll introduce you to her whenever you feel inclined.'

He recited, very fast: 'She is the wife of V., the painter, a school friend of mine who's made her abominally unhappy; she has fled from the conjugal establishment where her perfections had rendered her an impossible inmate; she is still beautiful, witty, and penniless; she lives in a boarding house in the rue Demours, where she pays eighty-five francs a month for bed and breakfast; she does writing jobs, anonymous feuilletons, newspaper snippets, addressing envelopes, gives English lessons at three francs an hour, and has never had a lover. You see that this particular lie is as disagreeable as the truth.'

I handed him the little lighted lamp and accompanied him to the top of the stairs. As he walked down them, the tiny flame shone upward on his pointed beard, with its slightly turned-up end, and tinged it red.

When I had had enough of getting him to tell me about Marco, I asked Paul Masson to take me to be introduced to her, instead of bringing her to the rue Jacob. He had told me in confidence that she was about twice my age and I felt it was proper for a young woman to make the journey to meet a lady who was not so young. Naturally, Paul Masson accompanied me to the rue Demours.

The boarding house where Madame Marco V. lived has been pulled down. About 1897, all that this villa retained of its former garden was a euonymous hedge, a gravel path, and a flight of five steps leading up to the door. The moment I entered the hall I felt depressed. Certain smells, not properly speaking cooking smells, but odors escaped from a kitchen, are appalling revelations of poverty. On the first floor, Paul Masson knocked on a door and the voice of Madame Marco invited us to come in. A perfect voice, neither too high nor too low, but gay and well-pitched. What a surprise! Madame Marco looked young, Madame Marco was pretty and wore a silk dress, Madame Marco had pretty eyes, almost black, and wide-open like a deer's. She had a little cleft at the tip of her nose, hair touched with henna and worn in a tight, sponge-like mass on the forehead like Queen Alexandra's and curled short on the nape in the so-called eccentric fashion of certain women painters or musicians.

She called me 'little Madame,' indicated that Masson had talked so much about me and my long hair, apologized, without overdoing it, for having no port and no sweets to offer me. With an unaffected gesture, she indicated the kind of place she lived in, and following the sweep of her hand, I took in the piece of plush that hid the one-legged table, the shiny upholstery of the only armchair, and the two little threadbare pancake-cushions of Algerian design on the two other chairs. There was also a certain rug on the floor. The mantelpiece served as a bookshelf.

'I've imprisoned the clock in the cupboard,' said Marco. 'But I swear it deserved it. Luckily, there's another cupboard I can use for my washing things. Don't you smoke?'

I shook my head, and Marco stepped into the full light to put a match to her cigarette. Then I saw that the silk dress was splitting at every fold. What little linen showed at the neck was very white. Marco and Masson smoked and chatted together; Madame Marco had grasped at once that I preferred listening to talking. I forced myself not to look at the wallpaper, with its old-gold and garnet stripes, or at the bed and its cotton damask bedspread.

'Do look at the little painting, over there,' Madame Marco said to me. 'It was done by my husband. It's so pretty that I've kept it. It's that little corner of Hyères, *you* remember, Masson.'

And I looked enviously at Marco, Masson, and the little picture, who had all three been in Hyères. Like most young things, I knew how to withdraw into myself, far away from people talking in the same room, then return to them with a sudden mental effort, then leave them again. Throughout my visit to Marco, thanks to her delicate tact which let me off questions and answers, I was able to come and go without stirring from my chair; I could observe or I could shut my eyes at will. I saw her just as she was and what I saw both delighted and distressed me. Though her well-set features were fine, she had what is called a coarse skin, slightly leathery and masculine, with red patches on the neck and below the ears. But, at the same time, I was ravished by the lively intelligence of her smile, by the shape of her doe's eyes and the unusually proud, yet completely unaffected carriage of her head. She looked less like a pretty woman than like one of those chiseled, clear-cut aristocratic men who adorned the eighteenth century and were not ashamed of being handsome. Masson told me later she was extraordinarily like her grandfather, the Chevalier de St-Georges, a brilliant forebear who has no place in my story.

We became great friends, Marco and I. And after she had finished her Indian novel – it was rather like *La Femme qui tue*, as specified by the man who got paid ten sous a line – Monsieur Willy soothed Marco's sensitive feelings by asking her to do some research on condition she accepted a small fee. He even consented, when I urgently asked him to, to put in an appearance when she and I had a meal together. I had only to watch her to learn the most impeccable table manners. Monsieur Willy was always professing his love of good breeding; he found something to satisfy it in Marco's charming manners and in her turn of mind, which was urbane but inflexible and slightly caustic. Had she been born twenty years later she would, I think, have made a good journalist. When the summer came, it was Monsieur Willy who proposed taking this extremely pleasant companion, so dignified in her poverty, along with us to a mountain village in Franche-Comté. The luggage she brought with her was heartrendingly light. But at that time,

I myself had very little money at my disposal, and we settled ourselves very happily on the single upper floor of a noisy inn. The wooden balcony and a wicker armchair were all that Marco needed; she never went for walks. She never wearied of the restfulness, of the vivid purple that evening shed on the mountains, of the great bowls of raspberries. She had traveled and she compared the valleys hollowed out by the twilight with other landscapes. Up there I noticed that the only mail Marco received consisted of picture postcards from Masson and 'Best wishes for a good holiday,' also on a postcard, from a fellow ghostwriter at the Bibliothèque Nationale.

As we sat under the balcony awning on those hot afternoons, Marco mended her underclothes. She sewed badly, but conscientiously, and I flattered my vanity by giving her pieces of advice, such as: 'You're using too coarse a thread for fine needles . . . You shouldn't put blue baby ribbon in chemises, pink is much prettier in lingerie and up against the skin.' It was not long before I gave her others, concerning her face powder, the color of her lipstick, a hard line she penciled around the edge of her beautifully shaped eyelids. 'D'you think so? D'you think so?' she would say. My youthful authority was adamant. I took the comb, I made a charming little gap in her tight, sponge-like fringe, I proved expert at softly shadowing her eyes and putting a faint pink glow high up on her cheekbones, near her temples. But I did not know what to do with the unattractive skin of her neck or with a long shadow that hollowed her cheek. That flattering glow I put on her face transformed it so much that I promptly wiped it off again. Taking to amber powder and being far better fed than in Paris had quite an animating effect. She told me about one of her former journeys when, like a good painter's wife, she had followed her husband from Greek village to Moroccan hamlet, washed his brushes, and fried aubergines and pimentos in his oil. She promptly left off sewing to have a cigarette, blowing the smoke out through nostrils as soft as some herbivorous animal's. But she only told me the names of places, not of friends, and spoke of discomforts, not of griefs, so I dared not ask her to tell more. The mornings she spent in writing the first chapters of a new novel, at one sou a line, which was being seriously held up by lack of documentation about the early Christians.

'When I've put in lions in the arena and a golden-haired virgin abandoned to the licentious soldiers and a band of Christians escaping in a storm,' said Marco, 'I shall come to the end of my personal erudition. So I shall wait for the rest till I get back to Paris.'

I have said: we became great friends. That is true, if friendship is confined to a rare smoothness of intercourse, preserved by studiously veiled precautions that blunt all sharp points and angles. I could only gain by imitating Marco and her 'well-bred' surface manner. Moreover, she aroused not the faintest distrust in me. I felt her to be straight as a die, disgusted by anything that could cause pain, utterly remote from all feminine rivalries. But though love laughs at difference in age, friendship, especially between two women, is more acutely conscious of it. This is particularly true when friendship is just beginning, and wants, like love, to have everything all at once. The country filled me with a terrible longing for running streams, wet fields, active idleness.

'Marco, don't you think it would be marvelous if we got up early tomorrow and spent the morning under the fir trees where there are wild cyclaments and purple mushrooms?'

Marco shuddered, and clasped her little hands together.

'Oh, no! Oh, no! Go off on your own and leave me out of it, you young mountain goat.'

I have forgotten to mention that, after the first week, Monsieur Willy had returned to Paris 'on business.' He wrote me brief notes, spicing his prose, which derived from Mallarmé and Félix Fénéon, with onomatopeic words in Greek letters, German quotations, and English terms of endearment.

So I climbed up alone to the firs and the cyclamens. There was something intoxicating to me in the contrast between burning sun and the still-nocturnal cold of the plants growing out of a carpet of moss. More than once, I thought I would not go back for the midday meal. But I did go back, on account of Marco, who was savoring the joy of rest as if she had twenty years' accumulation of weariness to work off. She used to rest with her eyes shut, her face pale beneath her powder, looking utterly exhausted, as if convalescing from an illness. At the end of the afternoon, 11 she would take a little walk along the road that, in passing through the village, hardly left off being a delicious, twisting forest path that rang crisply under one's feet.

You must not imagine that the other 'tourists' were much more active than we were. People of my age will remember that a summer in the country, around 1897, bore no resemblance to the gadabout holidays of today. The most energetic walked as far as a pure, icy, slate-colored stream, taking with them camp stools, needlework, a novel, a picnic lunch, and useless fishing rods. On moonlit nights, girls and young men would go off in groups after dinner, which was served at seven, wander along the road, then return, stopping to wish each other good night. 'Are you thinking of bicycling as far as Saut-de-Giers tomorrow?' 'Oh, we're not making any definite plans. It all depends on the weather.' The men wore low-cut waistcoats like cummerbunds, with two rows of buttons and sham buttonholes, under a black or cream alpaca jacket, and check caps or straw hats. The girls and the young women were plump and well nourished, dressed in white linen or ecru tussore. When they turned up their sleeves, they displayed white arms, and under their big hats, their scarlet sunburn did not reach as high as their foreheads. Venturesome families went in for what was called 'bathing' and set off in the afternoons to immerse themselves at a spot where the stream broadened out, barely two and a half miles from the village. At night, around the communal dining table, the children's wet hair smelled of ponds and wild peppermint.

One day, so that I could read my mail, which was rich with two letters, an article cut out of *Art et Critique*, and some other odds and ends, Marco tactfully assumed her convalescent pose, shutting her eyes and leaning her head back against the fiber cushion of the wicker chair. She was wearing the ecru linen dressing gown that she put on to save the rest of her wardrobe when we were alone in our bedrooms or out on the wooden balcony. It was when she had on that dressing gown that she truly showed her age and the period to which she naturally belonged. Certain definite details, pathetically designed to flatter, typed her indelibly, such as a certain deliberate wave in her hair that emphasized the narrowness of her temples, a certain short fringe that would never allow itself to be combed the other way, the carriage of the chin imposed by a high, boned collar, the knees that were never parted and never crossed. Even the shabby dressing gown itself gave her away. Instead of resigning itself to the simplicity of a working garment, it was adorned with ruffles of imitation lace at the neck and wrists and a little frill around the hips.

Those tokens of a particular period of feminine fashion and behavior were just the very ones my own generation was in process of rejecting. The new 'angel' hairstyle and Cléo de Mérode's smooth swathes were designed to go with a boater worn like a halo, shirt blouses in the English style, and straight skirts. Bicycles and bloomers had swept victoriously through every class. I was beginning to be crazy about starched linen collars and rough woolens imported 13 from England. The split between the two fashions, the recent one and the very latest, was too blatantly obvious not to humiliate penniless women who delayed in adopting the one and abandoning the other. Occasionally frustrated in my own bursts of clothes-consciousness, I suffered for Marco, heroic in two worn-out dresses and two light blouses.

Slowly, I folded up my letters again, without my attention straying from the woman who was pretending to be asleep, the pretty woman of 1870 or 1875, who, out of modesty and lack of money, was giving up the attempt to follow us into 1898. In the uncompromising way of young women, I said to myself: 'If I were Marco, I'd do my hair like this, I'd dress like that.' Then I would make excuses for her: 'But she hasn't any money. If I had more money, I'd help her.'

Marco heard me folding up my letters, opened her eyes, and smiled. 'Nice mail?'

'Yes . . . Marco,' I said daringly, 'don't you have your letters sent on here?'

'Of course I do. All the correspondence I have is what you see me get.'

As I said nothing, she added, all in one burst: 'As you know, I'm separated from my husband. V.'s friends, thank heaven, have remained *his* friends and not mine. I had a child, twenty years ago, and I lost him when he was hardly more than a baby. And I've never had a lover. So you see, it's quite simple.'

'Never had a lover . . .' I repeated.

Marco laughed at my expression of dismay.

'Is that the thing that strikes you most? Don't be upset! That's the thing I've thought about least. In fact I've long ago given up thinking about it at all.'

My gaze wandered from her lovely eyes, rested by the pure air and the green of the chestnut groves, to the little cleft at the tip of her witty nose, to her teeth, a trifle discolored, but admirably sound and well set.

'But you're very pretty, Marco!'

'Oh!' she said gaily. 'I was even a charmer, once upon a time. Otherwise V. wouldn't have married me. To be perfectly frank with you, I'm convinced that fate has spared me one great trouble, the tiresome thing that's called a temperament. No, no, all that business of blood rushing into the cheeks, upturned eyeballs, palpitating nostrils, I admit I've never experienced it and never regretted it. You do believe me, don't you?'

'Yes,' I said mechanically, looking at Marco's mobile nostrils.

She laid her narrow hand on mine, with an impulsiveness that did not, I knew, come easily for her.

'A great deal of poverty, my child, and before the poverty the job of being an artist's wife in the most down-to-earth way . . . hard manual labor, next door to being a maid-of-all-work. I wonder where I should have found the time to be idle and well groomed and elegant in secret – in other words, to be someone's romantic mistress.'

She sighed, ran her hand over my hair, and brushed it back from my temples.

'Why don't you show the top part of your face a little? When I was young, I did my hair like that.'

As I had a horror of having my alley cat's temples exposed naked, I dodged away from the little hand and interrupted Marco, crying: 'No, you don't! No, you don't! *I'm* going to do *your* hair. I've got a marvelous idea!'

Brief confidences, the amusements of two women shut away from the world, hours that were now like those in a sewing room, now like the idle ones of convalescence – I do not remember that our pleasant holiday produced any genuine intimacy. I was inclined to feel deferent toward Marco, yet, paradoxically, to set hardly any store by her opinions on life and love. When she told me she might have been a mother, I realized that our friendly relationship would never be in the least like my passionate feeling for my real mother, nor would it ever approach the comradeship I should have had with a young woman. But at that time, I did not know any girl or woman of my own age with whom I could share a reckless gaiety, a mute complicity, a vitality that overflowed in fits of wild laughter, or with whom I could enjoy physical rivalries and rather crude pleasures that Marco's age, her delicate constitution, and her whole personality put out of her range and mine.

We talked, and we also read. I had been an insatiable reader in my childhood. Marco had educated herself. At first, I thought I could delve into Marco's well-stored mind and memory. But I noticed that she replied with a certain lassitude, and as if mistrustful of her own words.

'Marco, why are you called Marco?'

'Because my name is Léonie,' she answered. 'Léonie wasn't the right sort of name for V.'s wife. When I was twenty, V. made me pose in a tasseled Greek cap perched over one ear and Turkish slippers with long turned-up points. While he was painting, he used to sing this old sentimental ballad:

> *Fair Marco, do you love to dance*
> *In brilliant ballrooms, gay with flowers?*
> *Do you love, in night's dark hours,*
> *Ta ra ra, ta ra ra ra . . .*

I have forgotten the rest.'

I had never heard Marco sing before. Her voice was true and thin, clear as the voice of some old men.

'They were still singing that in my youth,' she said. 'Painters' studios did a great deal for the propagation of bad music.'

She seemed to want to preserve nothing of her past but a superficial irony. I was too young to realize what this calmness of hers implied. I had not yet learned to recognize the modesty of renunciation.

Toward the end of our summer holiday in Franche-Comté, something astonishing did, however, happen to Marco. Her husband, who was painting in the United

States, sent her, through his solicitor, a check for fifteen thousand francs. The only comment she made was to say, with a laugh: 'So he's actually got a solicitor now? Wonders will never cease!'

Then she returned the check and the solicitor's letter to their envelope and paid no more attention to them. But at dinner, she gave signs of being a trifle excited, and asked the waitress in a whisper if it was possible to have champagne. We had some. It was sweet and tepid and slightly corked and we only drank half the bottle between us.

Before we shut the communicating door between our rooms, as we did every night, Marco asked me a few questions. She wore an absent-minded expression as she inquired: 'Do you think people will be still wearing those wide-sleeved velvet coats next winter, you know the kind I mean? And where did you get that charming hat you had in the spring – with the brim sloping like a roof? I liked it immensely – on *you*, of course.'

She spoke lightly, hardly seeming to listen to my replies, and I pretended not to guess how deeply she had hidden her famished craving for decent clothes and fresh underlinen.

The next morning, she had regained control of herself.

'When all's said and done,' she said, 'I don't see why I should accept this sum from that . . . in other words, from my husband. If it pleases him at the moment to offer me charity, like giving alms to a beggar, that's no reason for me to accept it.'

As she spoke, she kept pulling out some threads the

laundress had torn in the cheap lace that edged her dressing gown. Where it fell open, it revealed a chemise that was more than humble. I lost my temper and I scolded Marco as an older woman might have chided a small girl. So much so that I felt a little ashamed, but she only laughed.

'There, there, don't get cross! Since you want me to, I'll allow myself to be kept by his lordship V. It's certainly my turn.'

I put my cheek against Marco's cheek. We stayed watching the harsh, reddish sun reaching the zenith and drinking up all the shadows that divided the mountains. The bend of the river quivered in the distance. Marco sighed.

'Would it be very expensive, a pretty little corset belt all made of ribbon, with rococo roses on the ends of the suspenders?'

The return to Paris drove Marco back to her novelette. Once again I saw her hat with the three blue thistles, her coat and skirt whose black was faded and pallid, her dark gray gloves, and her schoolgirl satchel of cardboard masquerading as leather. Before thinking of her personal elegance, she wanted to move to another place. She took a year's lease of a furnished flat; two rooms and a place where she could wash, plus a sort of cupboard-kitchen, on the ground floor. It was dark there in broad daylight but the red and white cretonne curtains and bedspread were not too hopelessly shabby. Marco nourished herself at midday in a little restaurant near the library and had tea and bread-and-butter at home at night except when I managed to keep her at my flat for a meal at which stuffed olives and rollmops replaced soup and roast meat. Sometimes Paul Masson brought along an excellent chocolate 'Quillet' from Quillet's, the cake shop in the rue de Buci.

Completely resigned to her task, Marco had so far acquired nothing except, as October turned out rainy, a kind of rubberized hooded cloak that smelled of asphalt. One day she arrived, her eyes looking anxious and guilty.

'There,' she said bravely, 'I've come to be scolded. I think I bought this coat in too much of a hurry. I've got the feeling that . . . that it's not quite right.'

I was amused by her being as shy as if she were my junior, but I stopped laughing when I had a good look at the coat. An unerring instinct led Marco, so discriminating in other ways, to choose bad material, deplorable cut, fussy braid.

The very next day, I took time off to go out with her and choose a wardrobe for her. Neither she nor I could aspire to the great dress houses, but I had the pleasure of seeing Marco looking slim and years younger in a dark tailor-made and in a navy serge dress with a white front. With the straight little caracul topcoat, two hats, and some under-clothes, the bill, if you please, came to fifteen hundred francs: you can see that I was ruthless with the funds sent by the painter V.

I might well have had something to say against Marco's hairstyle. But just that very season, there was a changeover to shorter hair and a different way of doing it, so that Marco was able to look as if she was ahead of fashion. In this I sincerely envied her, for whether I twisted it around my head 'à la Ceres' or let it hang to my skirt hem – 'like a well cord' as Jules Renard said – my long hair blighted my existence.

At this point, the memory of a certain evening obtrudes itself. Monsieur Willy had gone out on business somewhere, leaving Marco, Paul Masson, and myself alone together after dinner. When the three of us were on our own, we automatically became clandestinely merry, slightly childish, and, as it were, reassured. Masson would sometimes read aloud the serial in a daily paper, a novelette inexhaustibly rich in haughty titled ladies, fancy-dress balls in winter gardens, chaises dashing along 'at a triple gallop' drawn by pure-bred steeds, maidens pale but resolute, exposed to a thousand perils. And we used to laugh wholeheartedly.

'Ah!' Marco would sigh, 'I shall never be able to do as well as that. In the novelette world, I shall never be more than a little amateur.'

'Little amateur,' said Masson one night, 'here's just what you want. I've culled it from the Agony Column: "Man of letters bearing well-known name would be willing to assist young writers both sexes in early stages career." '

'Both sexes!' said Marco. 'Go on, Masson! I've only got one sex and, even then, I think I'm exaggerating by half.'

'Very well, I will go on,' said Masson. 'I will go on to

lieutenant (regular army), garrisoned near Paris, warm-hearted, cultured, wishes to maintain correspondence with intelligent, affectionate woman. Very good, but apparently, this soldier does not wish to maintain anything but correspondence. Nevertheless, do we write to him? Let us write. The best letter wins a box of Gianduja Kohler – the nutty kind.'

'If it's a big box,' I said, 'I'm quite willing to compete. What about you, Marco?'

With her cleft nose bent over a scribbling block, Marco was writing already. Masson gave birth to twenty lines in which sly obscenity vied with humor. I stopped after the first page, out of laziness. But how charming Marco's letter was!

'First prize!' I exclaimed.

'Pearls before . . .' muttered Masson. 'Do we send it? Poste Restante, Alex 2, Box 59. Give it to me. I'll see that it goes.'

'After all, I'm not risking anything,' said Marco.

When our diversions were over, she slipped on her mackintosh again and put on her narrow hat in front of the mirror. It was a hat I had chosen, which made her head look very small and her eyes very large under its turned-down brim.

'Look at her!' she exclaimed. 'Look at her, the middle-aged lady who debauches warmhearted and cultured lieutenants!'

With the little oil lamp in her hand, she preceded Paul

Masson.

'I shan't see you at all this week,' she told me. 'I've got two pieces of homework to do: the chariot race and the Christians in the lions' pit.'

'Haven't I already read something of the kind some-where?' put in Masson.

'I sincerely hope you have,' retorted Marco. 'If it hadn't been done over and over again, where should I get my documentation?'

The following week, Masson bought a copy of the paper and with his hard, corrugated nail pointed out three lines in the Agony Column: 'Alex 2 implores author delicious letter beginning "What presumption" to give address. Secrecy scrupulously honored.'

'Marco,' he said, 'you've won not only the box of Gianduja but also a booby prize in the shape of a first-class mug.'

Marco shrugged her shoulders.

'It's cruel, what you've made me do. He's sure to think he's been made fun of, poor boy.'

Masson screwed up his eyes to their smallest and most inquisitorial.

'Sorry for him already, dear?'

These memories are distant, but precise. They rise out of the fog that inevitably drowns the long days of that particular time, the monotonous amusements of dress rehearsals and suppers at Pousset's, my alterations between animal gaiety and confused unhappiness, the split in my nature between a wild, frightened creature and one with a vast capacity for illusion. But it is a fog that leaves the faces of my friends intact and shining clear.

It was also on a rainy night, in late October or early November, that Marco came to keep me company one night; I remember the anthracite smell of the waterproof cape. She kissed me. Her soft nose was wet, she sighed with pleasure at the sight of the glowing stove. She opened her satchel.

'Here, read this,' she said. 'Don't you think he's got a charming turn of phrase, this . . . this ruffianly soldier?'

If, after reading it, I had allowed myself a criticism, I should have said: too charming. A letter worked over and recopied; one draft, two drafts thrown into the wastepaper basket. The letter of a shy man, with a touch of the poet, like everyone else.

'Marco, you mean you actually wrote to him?'

The virtuous Marco laughed in my face.

'One can't hide anything from you, charming daughter of Monsieur de La Palisse! Written? Written more than once, even! Crime gives me an appetite. You haven't got a cake? Or an apple?'

While she nibbled delicately, I showed off my ideas on the subject of graphology.

'Look, Marco, how carefully your "ruffianly soldier" has covered up a word he's begun so as to make it illegible. Sign of gumption, also of touchiness. The writer, as

Crépieux-Jamin says, doesn't like people to laugh at him.'

Marco agreed, absentmindedly. I noticed she was looking pretty and animated. She studied herself in the glass, clenching her teeth and parting her lips, a grimace few women can resist making in front of a mirror when they have white teeth.

'Whatever's the name of that toothpaste that reddens the gums, Colette?'

'Cherry something or other.'

'Thanks, I've got it now. Cherry Dentifrice. Will you do me a favor? Don't tell Paul Masson about my epistolary escapades. He'd never stop teasing me. I shan't keep up my relations with the regular army long enough to make myself ridiculous. Oh, I forgot to tell you. My husband has sent me another fifteen thousand francs.'

'Mercy me, be I a-hearing right? as they say where I come from. And you just simply *forgot* that bit of news?'

'Yes, really,' said Marco. 'I just forgot.'

She raised her eyebrows with an air of surprise to remind me delicately that money is always a subject of minor importance.

From that moment, it seemed to me that everything moved very fast for Marco. Perhaps that was due to distance. One of my moves – the first – took me from the rue Jacob to the top of the rue de Courcelles, from a dark little cubbyhole to a studio whose great window let in cold, heat, and an excess of light. I wanted to show my sophistication, to satisfy my newly born – and modest – cravings for luxury: I bought white goatskins, and a folding shower bath from Chaboche's.

Marco, who felt at home in dim rooms and in the atmosphere of the Left Bank and of libraries, blinked her lovely eyes under the studio skylight, stared at the white divans that suggested polar bears, and did not like the new way I did my hair. I wore it pulled up above my forehead and twisted into a high chignon; this new 'helmet' fashion had swept the hair up from the most modest and retiring napes.

Such a minor domestic upheaval would not have been worth mentioning, did it not make it understandable that, for some time, I only had rapid glimpses of Marco. My pictures of her succeeded each other jerkily like the pictures in those children's books that, as you turn the pages fast, give the illusion of continuous movement. When she brought me the second letter from the romantic lieutenant, I had crossed the intervening gulf. As Marco walked into my new, light flat, I saw that she was definitely prettier than she had been the year before. The slender foot she thrust out below the hem of her skirt rejoiced in the kind of shoe it deserved. Through the veil stretched taut over the little cleft at the tip of her nose she stared, now at her gloved hand, now at each unknown room, but she seemed to see neither the one nor the other clearly. With bright patience she endured my arranging and rearranging the curtains: she admired the folding shower bath, which, when erected, vaguely suggested a vertical coffin.

She was so patient and so absentminded that in the end I noticed it and asked her crudely: 'By the way, Marco, how's the ruffianly soldier?'

Her eyes, softened by makeup and shortsightedness, looked into mine.

'As it happens, he's very well. His letters are charming – decidedly so.'

'Decidedly so? How many have you had?'

'Three in all. I'm beginning to think it's enough. Don't you agree?'

'No, since they're charming – and they amuse you.'

'I don't care for the atmosphere of the *poste restante* . . . It's a horrid hole. Everyone there has a guilty look. Here, if you're interested . . .'

She threw a letter into my lap; it had been there ready all the time, folded up in her gloved hand. I read it rather slowly, I was so preoccupied with its serious tone, devoid of the faintest trace of humor.

'What a remarkable lieutenant you've come across, Marco! I'm sure that if he weren't restrained by his shyness . . .'

'His shyness?' protested Marco. 'He's already got to the point of hoping that we shall exchange less impersonal letters! What cheek! For a shy man . . .'

She broke off to raise her veil which was overheating her coarse-grained skin and flushing up those uneven red patches on her cheeks. But nowadays she knew how to apply her powder cleverly, how to brighten the color of her mouth. Instead of a discouraged woman of forty-five, I saw before me a smart woman of forty, her chin held high above the boned collar that hid the secrets of the neck. Once again, because of her very beautiful eyes, I forgot the deterioration of all the rest of her face and sighed inwardly: 'What a pity . . .'

Our respective moves took us away from our old surroundings and I did not see Marco quite so often. But she was very much in my mind. The polarity of affection between two women friends that gives one authority and the other pleasure in being advised turned me into a peremptory young guide. I decided that Marco ought to wear shorter skirts and more nipped-in waistlines. I sternly rejected braid, which made her look old, colors that dated her, and, most of all, certain hats that, when Marco puts them on, mysteriously sentenced her beyond hope of appeal. She allowed herself to be persuaded, though she would hesitate for a moment: 'You think so? You're quite sure?' and glance at me out of the corner of her beautiful eye.

We liked meeting each other in a little tearoom at the corner of the rue de l'Échelle and the rue d'Argenteuil, a warm, poky 'British,' saturated with the bitter smell of Ceylon tea. We 'partook of tea,' like other sweet-toothed ladies of those far-off days, and hot buttered toast followed by quantities of cakes. I liked my tea very black, with a thick white layer of cream and plenty of sugar. I believed I was learning English when I asked the waitress: 'Edith, please, a little more milk, and butter.'

It was at the little 'British' that I perceived such a change in Marco that I could not have been more startled if, since our last meeting, she had dyed her hair peroxide or taken to drugs. I feared some danger, I imagined that the wretch of a husband had frightened her into his clutches again. But if she was frightened, she would not have had that blank flickering gaze that wandered from the table to the walls and was profoundly indifferent to everything it glanced at.

'Marco? Marco?'

'Darling?'

'Marco, what on earth's happened? Have other treasure galleons arrived? Or what?'

She smiled at me as if I were a stranger.

'Galleons? Oh, no.'

She emptied her cup in one gulp and said almost in a whisper: 'Oh, how stupid of me, I've burned myself.'

Consciousness and affection slowly returned to her gaze. She saw that mine was astonished and she blushed, clumsily and unevenly, as she always did.

'Forgive me,' she said, laying her little hand on mine.

She sighed and relaxed.

'Oh!' she said. 'What luck there isn't anyone here. I'm a little . . . how can I put it? . . . queasy.'

'More tea? Drink it very hot.'

'No, no. I think it's that glass of port I had before I came here. No, nothing, thanks.'

She leaned back in her chair and closed her eyes. She was wearing her newest suit, a little oval brooch of the 'family heirloom' type was pinned at the base of the high boned collar of her cream blouse. The next moment she had revived and was completely herself, consulting the mirror in her new handbag and feverishly anticipating my questions.

'Ah, I'm better now! It was that port, I'm sure it was. Yes, my dear, port! And in the company of Lieutenant Alexis Trallard, son of General Trallard.'

'Ah!' I exclaimed with relief, 'is *that* all? You quite frightened me. So you've actually seen the ruffianly soldier? What's he like? Is he like his letters? Does he stammer? Has he got a lisp? Is he bald? Has he a port-wine mark on his nose?'

These and similar idiotic suggestions were intended to make Marco laugh. But she listened to me with a dreamy, refined expression as she nibbled at a piece of buttered toast that had gone cold.

'My dear,' she said at last. 'If you'll let me get a word in edgewise, I might inform you that Lieutenant Trallard is neither an invalid nor a monster. Incidentally, I've known this ever since last week, because he enclosed a photograph in one of his letters.'

She took my hand.

'Don't be cross. I didn't dare mention it to you. I was afraid.'

'Afraid of what?'

'Of you, darling, of being teased a little. And . . . well . . .

just simply afraid!'

'But why *afraid*?'

She made an apologetic gesture of ignorance, clutching her arms against her breast.

'Here's the Object,' she said, opening her handbag. 'Of course, it's a very bad snapshot.'

'He's much better looking than the photo . . . of course?'

'Better looking . . . good heavens, he's totally *different*. Especially his expression.'

As I bent over the photograph, she bent over it too, as if to protect it from too harsh a judgment.

'Lieutenant Trallard hasn't got that shadow like a saber cut on his cheek. Besides, his nose isn't so long. He's got light brown hair and his mustache is almost golden.'

After a silence, Marco added shyly: 'He's tall.'

I realized it was my turn to say something.

'But he's very good-looking! But he looks exactly as a lieutenant should! But what an enchanting story, Marco! And his eyes? What are his eyes like?'

'Light brown like his hair,' said Marco eagerly.

She pulled herself together.

'I mean, that was my general impression. I didn't look very closely.'

I hid my astonishment at being confronted with a Marco whose words, whose embarrassment, whose naïveté surpassed the reactions of the greenest girl to being stood a glass of port by a lieutenant. I could never have believed that this middle-aged married woman, inured to living among 31 bohemians, was at heart a timorous novice. I restrained myself from letting Marco see, but I think she guessed my thoughts, for she tried to turn her encounter, her 'queasiness,' and her lieutenant into a joke. I helped her as best I could.

'And when are you going to see Lieutenant Trallard again, Marco?'

'Not for a good while, I think.'

'Why?'

'Why, because he must be left to wear his nerves to shreds in suspense! Left to simmer!' declared Marco, raising a learned forefinger. 'Simmer! That's my principle!'

We laughed at last; laughed a great deal and rather idiotically. That hour seems to me, in retrospect, like the last halt, the last landing on which my friend Marco stopped to regain her breath. During the days that followed I have a vision of myself writing (I did not sign my work either) on the thin, crackly American paper I liked best of all, and Marco was busy working too, at one sou a line. One afternoon, she came to see me again.

'Good news of the ruffianly soldier, Marco?'

She archly indicated 'Yes' with her chin and her eyes, because Monsieur Willy was on the other side of the glass-topped door. She submitted a sample of dress material which she would not dream of buying without my approval. She was buoyant and I thought that, like a sensible woman, she had reduced Lieutenant Alexis Trallard to his

proper status. But when we were all alone in my bedroom,

that refuge hung with rush matting that smelled of damp reeds, she held out a letter, without saying a word, and without saying a word, I read it and gave it back to her. For the accents of love inspire only silence and the letter I had read was full of love. Full of serious, vernal love. Why did one question, the very one I should have repressed, escape me? I asked – thinking of the freshness of the words I had just read, of the respect that permeated them – I asked indiscreetly: 'How old is he?'

Marco put her two hands over her face, gave a sudden sob, and whispered: 'Oh, heavens! It's appalling!'

Almost at once, she mastered herself, uncovered her face, and chided herself in a harsh voice: 'Stop this nonsense. I'm dining with him tonight.'

She was about to wipe her wet eyes but I stopped her.

'Let me do it, Marco.'

With my two thumbs, I raised her upper eyelids so that the two tears about to fall should be reabsorbed and not smudge the mascara on her lashes by wetting them.

'There! Wait, I haven't finished.'

I retouched all her features. Her mouth was trembling a little. She submitted patiently, sighing as if I were dressing a wound. To complete everything, I filled the puff in her handbag with a rosier shade of powder. Neither of us uttered a word meanwhile.

'Whatever happens,' I told her, 'don't cry. At all costs, don't let yourself give way to tears.'

She jibbed at this, and laughed.

'All the same, we haven't got to the scene of the final parting yet!'

I took her over to the best-lighted looking glass. At the sight of her reflection, the corners of Marco's mouth quivered a little.

'Satisfied with the effect, Marco?'

'Too good to be true.'

'Can't ever be too good. You'll tell me what happened? When?'

'As soon as I know myself,' said Marco.

Two days later, she returned, in spite of stormy, almost warm weather that rattled the cowls on the chimney pots and beat back the smoke and fumes of the slow-combustion stove.

'Outdoors in this tempest, Marco?'

'It doesn't worry me a bit, I've got a four-wheeler waiting down there.'

'Wouldn't you rather dine here with me?'

'I can't,' she said, averting her head.

'Right. But you can send the growler away. It's only half past six, you've plenty of time.'

'No, I haven't time. How does my face look?'

'Quite all right. In fact, very nice.'

'Yes, but . . . Quick, be an angel! Do what you did for me the day before yesterday. And then, what's the best thing to receive Alex at home in? Outdoor clothes, don't you think? Anyway, I haven't got an indoor frock that would really do.'

'Marco, you know just as well as I do . . .'

'No,' she broke in, 'I don't know. You might as well tell me I know India because I've written a novelette that takes place in the Punjab. Look, he's sent a kind of emergency supply around to my place – a cold chicken in aspic, champagne, some fruit. He says that, like me, he has a horror of restaurants. Ah, now I think of it, I *ought* to have . . .'

She pressed her hand to her forehead, under her fringe.

'I *ought* to have bought that black dress last Saturday – the one I saw in the secondhand shop. Just my size, with a Liberty silk skirt and a lace top. Tell me, could you possibly lend me some very fine stockings? I've left it too late now to . . .'

'Yes, yes, of course.'

'Thank you. Don't you think a flower to brighten up my dress? No, *not* a flower on the bodice. Is it true that iris is a scent that's gone out of fashion? I'm sure I had heaps of other things to ask you . . . heaps of things.'

Though she was in the shelter of my room, sitting by the roaring stove, Marco gave me the impression of a woman battling with the wind and the rain that lashed the glass panes. I seemed to be watching Marco set off on some kind of journey, embarking like an emigrant. It was as if I could see a flapping cape blowing around her, a plaid scarf streaming in the wind.

Besieged, soon to be invaded. There was no doubt in my mind that an attack was being launched against the most defenseless of creatures. Silent, as if we were committing a crime, we hurried through our beauty operations. Marco attempted to laugh.

'We're trampling the most rigorously established customs underfoot. Normally, it's the oldest witch who washes and decks the youngest for the Sabbath.'

'Ssh, Marco, keep still – I've just about finished.'

I rolled up the pair of silk stockings in a piece of paper, along with a little bottle of yellow Chartreuse.

'Have you got any cigarettes at home?'

'Yes. Whatever am I saying? No. But *he'll* have some on him, he smokes Egyptian ones.'

'I'll put four amusing little napkins in the parcel, it'll make it more like a doll's dinner party. Would you like the cloth too?'

'No, thanks. I've got an embroidered one I bought ages ago in Brussels.'

We were talking in low, rapid whispers, without ever smiling. In the doorway, Marco turned around to give me a long, distracted look out of moist, made-up eyes, a look in which I could read nothing resembling joy. My thoughts followed her in the cab that was carrying her through the dark and the rain, over the puddle-drenched road where the wind blew miniature squalls around the lampposts. I wanted to open the window to watch her drive away but the whole tempestuous night burst into the studio and I shut it again on this traveler who was setting off on a dangerous voyage, with no ballast but a pair of silk stockings, some pink makeup, some fruit, and a bottle of champagne.

Lieutenant Trallard was still only relatively real to me, although I had seen his photograph. A very French face, a rather long nose, a well-chiseled forehead, hair *en brosse* and the indispensable mustache. But the picture of Marco blotted out his – Marco all anxious apprehension, her beauty enhanced by my tricks, and breathing fast, as a deer pants when it hears the hooves and clamor of the distant hunt. I listened to the wind and rain and I reckoned up her chances of crossing the sea and reaching port in safety. 'She was very pretty tonight. Provided her lamp with the pleated shade gives a becoming light. This young man preoccupies her, flatters her, peoples her solitude, in a word, rejuvenates her.'

A gust of bad weather beat furiously against the pane. A little black snake that oozed from the bottom of the window began to creep slowly along. From this, I realized that the window did not shut properly and the water was beginning to soak the carpet. I went off to seek floor cloths and the aid of Maria, the girl from Aveyron who was my servant at that time. On my way, I opened the door to Masson, who had just rung three times.

While he was diverting himself of a limp mackintosh cape that fell dripping on the tiled floor, like a basketful of eels, I exclaimed: 'Did you run into Marco? She's just this minute gone downstairs. She was so sorry not to see you.'

A lie must give off a smell that is apparent to people with sensitive nostrils. Paul Masson sniffed the air in my direction, curtly wagged his short beard, and went off to join Monsieur Willy in his white study that, with its brief curtains, beaded moldings, and small windowpanes, vaguely resembled a converted cake shop.

After that, everything progressed fast for Marco. Nevertheless she came back, after that stormy night, but she made me no confidences. It is true that a third person prevented them. That particular day, my impatience to know was restrained by the fear that her confidence might yield something that would have slightly horrified me; there was an indefinable air of furtiveness and guilt about her whole person. At least, that is what I *think* I remember. My memories, after that, are much more definite. How could I have forgotten that Marco underwent a magical transformation, the kind of belated, embarrassing puberty that deceives no one? She reacted violently to the slightest stimulus. A thimbleful of Frontignac set her cheeks and her eyes ablaze. She laughed for no reason, stared blankly into space, was incessantly resorting to her powder puff and her mirror. Everything was going at a great rate. I could not long put off the 'Well, Marco?' she must be waiting for.

One clear, biting winter night, Marco was with me. I was stoking up the stove. She kept her gaze fixed on its mica window and did not speak.

'Are you warm enough in your little flat, Marco? Does the coal grate give enough heat?'

She smiled vaguely, as if at a deaf person, and did not answer. So I said at last: 'Well, Marco? Contented? Happy?'

It was the last, the most important word, I think, that she pushed away with her hand.

'I did not believe,' she said, very low, 'that such a thing could exist.'

'What thing? Happiness?'

She flushed here and there, in dark, fiery patches. I asked her – it was my turn to be naïve: 'Then why don't you look more pleased?'

'Can one rejoice over something terrible, something that's so . . . so like an evil spell?'

I secretly permitted myself the thought that to use such a grim and weighty expression was, as the saying goes, to clap a very large hat on a very small head, and I waited for her next words. But none came. At this point, there was a brief period of silence. I saw nothing wrong in Marco's keeping quiet about her love affair: it was rather the love affair itself that I resented. I thought – unjust as I was and unmindful of her past – that she had been very quick to reward a casual acqaintance, even if he were an officer, a general's son, and had light brown hair into the bargain.

The period of reserve was followed by the season of unrestricted joy. Happiness, once accepted, is seldom reticent; Marco's, as it took firm root, was not very vocal but expressed itself in the usual boring way. I knew that, like every other woman, she had met a man 'absolutely unlike anyone else' and that everything he did was a source of abundant delight to his dazzled mistress. I was not allowed to remain ignorant that Alexis possessed a 'lofty soul' in addition to a 'cast-iron body.' Marco did not, thank heaven, belong to that tribe who boastfully whisper precise details – the sort of female I call a Madame-how-many-times. Nevertheless, by looking confused or by spasms of perturbed reticence, she had a mute way of conveying things I would gladly have been dispensed from knowing.

This virtuous victim of belated love and suddenly awakened sensuality did not submit all at once to blissful immolation. But she could not escape the usual snares of her new condition, the most unavoidable of which is eloquence, both of speech and gesture.

The first few weeks made her thin and dry-lipped, with feverish, glittering eyes. 'A Rops!' Paul Masson said behind her back. 'Madame Dracula,' said Monsieur Willy, going one better. 'What the devil can our worthy Marco be up to, to make her look like that?'

Masson screwed up his little eyes and shrugged one shoulder. 'Nothing,' he said coldly. 'These phenomena belong to neurotic simulation, like imaginary pregnancy. Probably, like many women, our worthy Marco imagines she is the bride of Satan. It's the phase of infernal joys.'

I thought it detestable that either of her two friends should call Madame V. 'our worthy Marco.' Nor was I any more favorably impressed by the icily critical comments of these two disillusioned men, especially on anything concerning friendship, esteem, or love.

Then Marco's face became irradiated with a great serenity. As she regained her calm, she gradually lost the fevered glitter of a lost soul and put on a little flesh. Her skin seemed smoother, she had lost the breathlessness that betrayed her nervousness and her haste. Her slightly increased weight slowed down her walk and movements; she smoked cigarettes lazily.

'New phase,' announced Masson. 'Now she looks like the Marco of the old days, when she'd just got married to V. It's the phase of the odalisque.'

I now come to a period when, because I was going about more and was also more loaded up with work, I saw Marco only at intervals. I dared not drop in on Marco without warning, for I dreaded I might encounter Lieutenant Trallard, only too literally in undress, in the minute flat that had nothing in the way of an entrance hall. What with teas put off and appointments broken, fate kept us apart, till at last it brought us together again in my studio, on a lovely June day that blew warm and cool breezes through the open window.

Marco smelled delicious. Marco was wearing a brand-new black dress with white stripes, Marco was all smiles. Her romantic love affair had already been going on for eight months. She looked so much fatter to me that the proud carriage of her head no longer preserved her chin line and her waist, visibly compressed, no longer moved flexibly inside the petersham belt, as it had done last year.

'Congratulations, Marco! You look marvelously well!'

Her long deer's eyes looked uneasy.

'You think I've got plump? Not too plump, I hope?'

She lowered her lids and smiled mysteriously. 'A little extra flesh does make one's breasts so pretty.'

I was not used to that kind of remark from her and I was the one who felt embarrassed, frankly, as embarrassed as if Marco – that very Marco who used to barricade herself in her room at the country inn, crying: 'Don't come in, I'll slip on my dressing gown!' – had deliberately stripped naked in the middle of my studio drawing room.

The next second, I told myself I was being ungenerous and unfriendly, that I ought to rejoice wholeheartedly in Marco's happiness. To prove my goodwill, I said gaily: 'I bet, one of these days, when I open the door to you, I'll find Lieutenant Trallard in your wake! I'm too magnanimous to refuse him a cup of tea and a slice of bread and cheese, Marco. So why not bring him along next time?'

Marco gave me a sharp look that was like a total stranger's. Quickly as she averted it, I could not miss the virulent, suspicious glance that swept over me, over my smile and my long hair, over everything that youth lavishes on a face and body of twenty-five.

'No,' she said.

She recovered herself and looked back at me with her usual doe-like gentleness.

'It's too soon,' she said gracefully. 'Let's wait till the "ruffianly soldier" deserves such an honor!'

But I remained appalled at having caught, in one look, a glimpse of a primitive female animal, black with suspicion, hostility, and possessive passion. For the first time, we were both aware of the difference in our ages as something sharp, cruel, and irremediable. It was the difference in age, revealed in the depths of a beautiful velvety eye, that falsified our relationship and disrupted our old bond. When I saw Marco again after the 'day of the look' and I inquired after Lieutenant Trallard, the new-style Marco, plump, white, calm – almost matriarchal – answered me in a tone of false modesty, the tone of a greedy and sated proprietress. I stared at her, stupefied, looking for all the things of which voracious, unhoped-for love had robbed her. I looked in vain for her elegant thinness, for the firmness of her slender waist, for her rather bony, well-defined chin, for the deep hollows in which the velvety, almost black eyes used to shelter . . . Realizing that I was registering the change in her, she renounced the dignity of a well-fed sultana and became uneasy.

'What can I do about it? I'm putting on weight.'

'It's only temporary,' I said. 'Do you eat a lot?'

She shrugged her thickened shoulders.

'I don't know. Yes. I *am* more greedy, that's a fact, than . . . than before. But I've often seen you eat enormously and *you* don't put on weight!'

To exonerate myself, I made a gesture to signify that I couldn't help this. Marco stood up, planted herself in front of the mirror, clutched her waist tightly with both hands, and kneaded it.

'Last year you weren't happy, Marco.'

'Oh, so that's it!' she said bitterly.

She was studying her reflection at close quarters as if she were alone. The addition of some few pounds had turned her into another woman, or rather another type of woman. The flesh was awkwardly distributed on her lightly built frame. 'She's got a behind like a cobbler's,' I thought. In my part of the country, they say that the cobbler's behind gets flat from sitting so much but develops a square shape. 'And, in addition, breasts like jellyfish, very broad and decidedly flabby.' For even if she is fond of her, a woman always judges another woman harshly.

Marco turned around abruptly.

'What was that?' she asked.

'I didn't say anything, Marco.'

'Sorry. I thought you did.'

'If you really want to fight against a tendency to put on flesh . . .'

'*Tendency*,' Marco echoed, between her teeth. 'Tendency is putting it mildly.'

'. . . why don't you try Swedish gymnastics? People are talking a lot about them.'

She interrupted me with a gesture of intolerant refusal.

'Or else cut out breakfast? In the morning don't have anything but unsweetened lemon juice in a glass of water.'

'But I'm hungry in the morning!' cried Marco. 'Everything's different, do realize that! I'm hungry, I wake up thinking of fresh butter – and thick cream – and coffee, and ham. I think that, after breakfast, there'll be luncheon to follow and I think of . . . of what will come after luncheon, the thing that kindles this hunger again – and all these cravings I have now that are so terribly fierce.'

Dropping her hands that had been harshly pummeling her waist and bosom, she challenged me in the same querulous tone: 'Candidly, could *I* ever have foreseen . . .'

Her voice changed. 'He actually says that I make him so happy.'

I could not resist putting my arms around her neck.

'Marco, don't worry about so many things! What you've just said explains everything, justifies everything. Be happy, Marco, make him happy and let everything else go hang!'

We kissed each other. She went away reassured, swaying on those unfamiliar broadened hips. Soon afterward, Monsieur Willy and I went off to Bayreuth and I did not fail to send Marco a great many picture postcards, covered with Wagnerian emblems entwined with leitmotifs. As soon as I returned, I asked Marco to meet me at our tearoom. She had not grown any thinner nor did she look any younger. Where others develop curves and rotundity, Marco's fleshiness tended to be square.

'And you haven't been away from Paris at all, Marco? Nothing's changed?'

'Nothing, thank God.'

She touched the wood of the little table with the tip of her finger to avert ill luck. I needed nothing but that gesture to tell me that Marco still belonged, body and soul, to Lieutenant Trallard. Another, no less eloquent sign was that Marco only asked me questions of pure politeness about my stay in Bayreuth – moreover, I guessed she did not even listen to my answers.

She blushed when I asked her, in my turn: 'What about work, Marco? Any novelettes on the stocks for next season?'

'Oh, nothing much,' she said in a bored voice. 'A publisher wants a novel for children of eight to fourteen. As if that was up my street! Anyway . . .'

A gentle, cowlike expression passed over her face like a cloud and she closed her eyes.

'Anyway, I feel so lazy . . . oh, *so* lazy!'

When Masson, informed of our return, announced himself with his usual three rings, he hastened to tell me he knew 'all' from Marco's own lips. To my surprise, he spoke favorably of Lieutenant Trallard. He did not take the line that he was a tenth-rate gigolo or a drunkard destined to premature baldness or a garrison-town Casanova. On the other hand, I thought he was decidedly harsh about Marco and even more cold than harsh.

'But, come now, Paul, what are you blaming Marco for in this affair?'

'Pooh! nothing,' said Paul Masson.

'And they're madly happy together, you know!'

'Madly strikes me as no exaggeration.'

He gave a quiet little laugh that was echoed by Monsieur Willy. Detestable laughs that made fun of Marco and myself, and were accompanied by blunt opinions and pessimistic forecasts, formulated with complete assurance and indifference, as if the romance that lit up Marco's Indian summer were no more than some stale bit of gossip.

'Physically,' Paul Masson said, 'Marco *had* reached the phase known as the brewer's dray horse. When a gazelle turns into a brood mare, it's a bad lookout for her. Lieutenant Trallard was perfectly right. It was Marco who compromised Lieutenant Trallard.'

'Compromised? You're crazy, Masson! Honestly, the things you say.'

'My dear girl, a child of three would tell you, as I do, that Marco's first, most urgent duty was to remain slender, charming, elusive, a twilight creature beaded with rain-drops, not to be bursting with health and frightening people in the streets by shouting: "I've done it! I've done it! I've . . ." '

'Masson!'

My blood was boiling; I flogged Masson with my rope of hair. I understood nothing of that curious kind of severity only men display toward an innocence peculiar to women. I listened to the judgments of these two on the 'Marco case,' judgments that admitted not one extenuating circumstance, as if they were lecturing on higher mathematics.

'She *wasn't* up to it,' decreed one of them. 'She fondly supposed that being the forty-six-year-old mistress of a young man of twenty-five was a delightful adventure.'

'Whereas it's a profession,' said the other.

'Or rather, a highly skilled sport.'

'No. Sport is an unpaid job. But she wouldn't even

understand that her one and only hope is to break it off.'

I had not yet become inured to the mixture of affected cynicism and literary paradox by which, around 1900, intelligent, bitter, frustrated men maintained their self-esteem.

September lay over Paris, a September of fine, dry days and crimson sunsets. I sulked over being in town and over my husband's decision to cut short my summer holiday. One day, I received an express letter that I stared at in surprise, for I did not know Marco's writing well. The handwriting was regular but the spaces between the letters betrayed emotional agitation. She wanted to talk to me. I was in, waiting for her, at the hour when the red light from the setting sun tinged the yellow-curtained windowpane with a vinous flush. I was pleased to see there was no outward trace of disturbance about her. As if there were no other possible subject of conversation, Marco announced at once: 'Just imagine, Alex is going off on a mission.'

'On a mission? Where to?'

'Morocco.'

'When?'

'Almost at once. Perhaps in a week's time. Orders from the War Office.'

'And there's no way out of it?'

'His father, General Trallard . . . yes, if his father intervened personally, he might be able . . . But he thinks this mission – incidentally, it's quite a dangerous one – is a great honor. So . . .'

She made a little, abortive gesture and fell silent, staring into vacancy. Her heavy body, her full, pale cheeks and stricken eyes made her look like a tragedy queen.

'Does a mission take a long time, Marco?'

'I don't know – I haven't the faintest idea. He talks of three or four months, possibly five.'

'Now, now, Marco,' I said gaily. 'What's three or four months? You'll wait for him, that's all.'

She did not seem to hear me. She seemed to be attentively studying a purple-ink cleaner's mark on the inside of her glove.

'Marco,' I risked, 'couldn't you go over there with him and live in the same district?'

The moment I spoke, I regretted it. Marco, with trunks full of dresses, Marco as the European favorite, or else Marco as the native wife going in for silver bangles, couscous, and fringed scarves. The pictures my imagination conjured up made me afraid – afraid for Marco.

'Of course,' I hastily added, 'that wouldn't be practical.'

Night was falling and I got up to give us some light, but Marco restrained me.

'Wait,' she said. 'There's something else. I'd rather not talk to you about it here. Will you come to my place tomorrow? I've got some good China tea and some little salted cakes from the boulevard Malesherbes.'

'Of course I'd love to, Marco! But . . .'

'I'm not expecting anyone tomorrow. Do come, you might be able to do me a great service. Don't put on the 49 light, the light in the hall is all I need.'

Marco's little 'furnished suite' had changed too. An arrangement of curtains on a wooden frame behind the entrance door provided it with a substitute for a hall. The brass bedstead had become a divan-bed and various new pieces of furniture struck me quite favorably, as also did some Oriental rugs. A garlanded Venetian glass over the mantelpiece reflected some red and white dahlias. In the scent that pervaded it, I recognized Marco's married, if I can use the expression, to another, full-bodied fragrance.

The second, smaller room served as a bathroom; I caught sight of a zinc bathtub and a kind of shower arrangement fixed to the ceiling. I made, as I came in, some obvious remark such as: 'How nice you've made it here, Marco!'

The stormy, precociously cold September day did not penetrate into this confined dwelling, whose thick walls and closed windows kept the air perfectly still. Marco was already busy getting tea, setting out our two cups and our two plates. 'She's not expecting anyone,' I thought. She offered me a saucer full of greengages while she warmed the teapot.

'What beautiful little hands you have, Marco!'

She suddenly knocked over a cup, as if the least unexpected sound upset the conscious control of her movements. We went through that pretense of a meal that covers and puts off the embarrassment of explanations, rifts, and silences; nevertheless, we reached the moment when Marco had to say what she wanted to say. It was indeed high time; I could see she was almost at the end of her tether. We instinctively find it odd, even comic, when a plump person shows signs of nervous exhaustion and I was surprised that Marco could be at once so buxom and in such a state of collapse. She pulled herself together; I saw her face, once again, look like a noble warrior's. The cigarette she avidly lit after tea completed her recovery. The glint of henna on her short hair suited her.

'Well,' she began in a clear voice, 'I think it's over.'

No doubt she had not planned to open with those words, for she stopped, as if aghast.

'Over? Why, what's over?'

'You know perfectly well what I mean,' she said. 'If you're at all fond of me, as I think you are, you'll try and help me, but . . . All the same, I'm going to tell you.'

Those were almost her last coherent words. In putting down the story that I heard, I am obliged to cut out all that made it, in Marco's version, so confused and so terribly clear.

She told it as many women do, going far back, and irrelevantly, into the past of what had been her single, dazzling love affair. She kept on repeating herself and correcting dates: 'So it must have been Thursday, December 26. What *am* I saying? It was a Friday, because we'd been to Prunier's to have a fish dinner. He's a practicing Catholic and abstains on Fridays.'

Then the detailed minuteness of the story went to pieces.

Marco lost the thread and kept breaking off to say, 'Oh well, we can skip that!' or 'Goodness, I can't remember where I'd got to!' and interlarding every other sentence with 'You know.' Grief drove her to violent gesticulation: she kept smiting her knees with the palm of her hand and flinging her head back against the chair cushions.

All the time she was running on with the prolixity and banality that give all lovers' laments a family likeness, accompanying certain indecent innuendoes with a pantomime of lowering her long eyelids. I felt completely unmoved. I was conscious only of a longing to get away and even had to keep clenching my jaws to repress nervous yawns. I found Marco all too tiresomely like every other woman in love; she was also taking an unconscionably long time to tell me how all this raving about a handsome young soldier came to end in disaster – a disaster, of course, totally unlike anyone else's; they always are.

'Well, one day . . .' said Marco, at long last.

She put her elbows on the arms of her chair. I imitated her and we both leaned forward. Marco broke off her confused jeremiad and I saw a gleam of awareness come into her soft, sad eyes, a look capable of seeing the truth. The tone of her voice changed too, and I will try to summarize the dramatic part of her story.

In the verbosity of the early stage, she had not omitted to mention the 'madness of passion,' the fiery ardor of the young man who would impetuously rush through the half-open door, pull aside the curtain, and, from there, make one bound onto the divan where Marco lay awaiting him. He could not endure wasting time in preliminaries or speeches. Impetuosity has its own particular ritual. Marco gave me to understand that, more often than not, the lieutenant, his gloves, and his peaked cap were all flung down haphazardly on the divan. Poetry and sweet nothings only came afterward. At this point in her story, Marco made a prideful pause and turned her gaze toward a beveled, nickel-plated photograph frame. Her silence and her gaze invited me to various conjectures, and perhaps to a touch of envy.

'Well, so one day . . .' said Marco.

A day of license, definitely. One of those rainy Paris days when a mysterious damp that dulls the mirrors and a strange craving to fling off clothes incites lovers to shut themselves up and turn day into night, 'one of those days,' Marco said, 'that are the perdition of body and soul . . .' I had to follow my friend and to imagine her – she forced me to – half naked on the divan bed, emerging from one of those ecstasies that were so crude and physical that she called them 'evil spells'. It was at that moment that her hand, straying over the bed, encountered the peaked forage cap known as a kepi and she yielded to one of those all-too-typical feminine reflexes; she sat up in her crumpled chemise, planted the kepi over one ear, gave it a roguish little tap to settle it, and hummed:

> With bugle and fife and drum
> The soldiers are coming to town . . .

53

'Never,' Marco told me, 'never have I seen anything like Alex's face. It was . . . incomprehensible. I'd say it was hideous, if he weren't so handsome . . . I can't tell you what my feelings were . . .'

She broke off and stared at the empty divan-bed.

'What happened then, Marco? What did he say?'

'Why, nothing. I took off the kepi, I got up, I tidied myself, we had some tea. In fact, everything passed off just as usual. But since that day I've two or three times caught Alex looking at me with that face again and with such a very odd expression in his eyes. I can't get rid of the idea that the kepi was fatal to me. Did it bring back some unpleasant memory? I'd like to know what *you* think. Tell me straight out, don't hedge.'

Before replying, I took care to compose my face; I was so terrified it might express the same horror, disapproval, and disgust as Lieutenant Trallard's. Oh, Marco! In one moment I destroyed you, I wept for you – I saw you. I saw you just as Alexis Trallard had seen you. My contemptuous eyes took in the slack breasts and the slipped shoulder straps of the crumpled chemise. And the leathery, furrowed neck, the red patches on the skin below the ears, the chin left to its own devices and long past hope. . . . And that groove, like a dried-up river, that hollows the lower eyelid after making love, and that vinous, fiery flush that does not cool off quickly enough when it burns on an aging face. And crowning all that, the kepi! The kepi – with its stiff lining and its jaunty peak, slanted over one roguishly winked eye.

'I know very well,' went on Marco, 'that between lovers, the slightest thing is enough to disturb a magnetic atmosphere . . . I know very well . . .'

Alas! What did she know?

'And after that, Marco? What was the end?'

'The end? But I've told you all there is to tell. Nothing else happened. The mission to Morocco turned up. The date's been put forward twice. But that isn't the only reason I've been losing sleep. Other signs . . .'

'What signs?'

She did not dare give a definite answer. She put out a hand as if to thrust away my question and averted her head.

'Oh, nothing, just . . . just differences.'

She strained her ears in the direction of the door.

'I haven't seen him for three days,' she said. 'Obviously he has an enormous amount to do getting ready for this mission. All the same . . .'

She gave a sidelong smile.

'All the same, I'm not a child,' she said in a detached voice. 'In any case, he writes to me. Express letters.'

'What are his letters like?'

'Oh, charming, of course, what else would they be? He may be very young but *he's* not quite a child either.'

As I stood up, Marco suddenly became anguished and humble and clutched my hands.

'What do you think I ought to do? What *does* one do in

55

these circumstances?'

'How can I possibly know, Marco? I think there's absolutely nothing to be done but to wait. I think it's essential, for your own dignity.'

She burst into an unexpected laugh.

'My dignity! Honestly, you make me laugh! My dignity! Oh, these young women.'

I found her laugh and her look equally unbearable.

'But, Marco, you're asking my advice – I'm giving it to you straight from the heart.'

She went on laughing and shrugging her shoulders. Still laughing, she brusquely opened the door in front of me. I thought that she was going to kiss me, that we should arrange another meeting, but I had hardly got outside before she shut the door behind me without saying anything beyond: 'My dignity! No, really, that's *too* funny!'

If I stick to facts, the story of Marco is ended. Marco had had a lover; Marco no longer had a lover. Marco had brought down the sword of Damocles by putting on the fatal kepi, and at the worst possible moment. At the moment when the man is a melancholy, still-vibrating harp, an explorer returning from a promised land, half-glimpsed but not attained, a lucid penitent swearing 'I'll never do it again' on bruised and bended knees.

I stubbornly insisted on seeing Marco again a few days later. I knocked and rang at her door, which was not opened. I went on and on, for I was aware of Marco there behind it, solitary, stony, and fevered. With my mouth to the keyhole, I said: 'It's Colette,' and Marco opened the door. I saw at once that she regretted having let me in. With an absentminded air, she kept stroking the loose skin of her small hands, smoothing it down toward the wrist like the cuff of a glove. I did not let myself be intimidated; I told her that I wanted her to come and dine with me at home that very night and that I wouldn't take no for an answer. And I took advantage of my authority to add: 'I suppose Lieutenant Trallard has left?'

'Yes,' said Marco.

'How long will it take him to get over there?'

'He isn't *over there*,' said Marco. 'He's at Ville d'Avray, staying with his father. It comes to the same thing.'

When I had murmured 'Ah!' I did not know what else to say.

'After all,' Marco went on, 'why shouldn't I come and have dinner with you?'

I made exclamations of delight, I thanked her. I behaved as effusively as a grateful fox terrier, without, I think, quite taking her in. When she was sitting in my room, in the warmth, under my lamp, in the glare of all that reflected whiteness, I could measure not only Marco's decline in looks but a kind of strange reduction in her. A diminution of weight – she was thinner – a diminution of resonance – she talked in a small, distinct voice. She must have forgotten to feed herself, and taken things to make herself sleep.

Masson came in after dinner. When he found Marco

there, he showed as much apprehension as his illegible face could express. He gave her a crab-like, sidelong bow.

'Why, it's Masson,' said Marco indifferently. 'Hello, Paul.'

They started up an old cronies' conversation, completely devoid of interest. I listened to them and I thought that such a string of bromides ought to be as good as a sleeping draught for Marco. She left early and Masson and I remained alone together.

'Paul, don't you think she looks ill, poor Marco?'

'Yes,' said Masson. 'It's the phase of the priest.'

'Of the . . . *what*?'

'The priest. When a woman, hitherto extremely feminine, begins to look like a priest, it's the sign that she no longer expects either kindness or ill treatment from the opposite sex. A certain yellowish pallor, something melancholy about the nose, a pinched smile, falling cheeks: Marco's a perfect example. The priest, I tell you, the priest.'

He got up to go, adding: 'Between ourselves, I prefer that in her to the odalisque.'

In the weeks that followed, I made a special point of not neglecting Marco. She was losing weight very fast indeed. It is difficult to hold on to someone who is melting away, it would be truer to say consuming herself. She moved house, that is to say, she packed her trunk and took it off to another little furnished flat. I saw her often, and never once did she mention Lieutenant Trallard. Then I saw her less often and the coolness was far more on her side than on mine. She seemed to be making a strange endeavor to turn herself into a shriveled little old lady. Time passed . . .

'But, Masson, what's happened to Marco? It's ages since . . . Have *you* any news of Marco?'

'Yes,' said Masson.

'And you haven't told me anything!'

'You haven't asked me anything.'

'Quick, where is she?'

'Almost every day at the Nationale. She's translated an extraordinary series of articles about the Ubangi from English into French. As the manuscript is a little short to make a book, she's making it longer at the publisher's request, and she's documenting herself at the library.'

'So she's taken up her old life again,' I said thoughtfully. 'Exactly as it was before Lieutenant Trallard . . .'

'Oh, no,' said Masson. 'There's a tremendous change in her existence!'

'What change? Really, one positively has to drag things out of you!'

'Nowadays,' said Masson, 'Marco gets paid two sous a line.'

[TRANSLATED BY ANTONIA WHITE]

A Note on Colette

Colette, creator of *Claudine, Chéri* and *Gigi*, is one of France's outstanding writers. She had a long, varied and active life. She was born in Burgundy in 1873, into a home overflowing with dogs, cats and children, and educated at the local village school. At the age of twenty she was brought to Paris by her first husband, the notorious Henry Gauthiers-Villars (Willy), writer and critic. Willy forced Colette to write her first novels (the Claudine sequence), which he published under his name. They were an instant success. But their marriage was never happy and Colette left him in 1906. She remarried (*Julie de Carneilhan* 'is as close a reckoning with the elements of her second marriage as she ever allowed herself'), later divorcing her second husband, by whom she had a daughter. In 1935 she married Maurice Goudeket, with whom she lived until her death in 1954.

With the publication of *Chéri* (1920) Colette's place as one of France's prose masters was assured. Her writing runs to fifteen volumes, novels, portraits, essays, *chroniques* and a large body of autobiographical prose. She was the first woman President of the Académie Goncourt, and